For Georgia - H.M.
For Eliza — S. M.

JF

First published in Great Britain in 2002 by
Frances Lincoln Limited, 4 Torriano Mews
Torriano Avenue, London NW5 2RZ

www.franceslincoln.com

British Library Cataloguing in Publication Data
available on request

ISBN 0-7112-1854-4

Set in Mrs Eaves

Printed in Singapore

1 3 5 7 9 8 6 4 2

DIARY of a PRINCESS

A Tale from Marco Polo's Travels

Heather Maisner

Illustrated by Sheila Moxley

FRANCES LINCOLN

Many centuries ago, the famous Venetian traveller Marco Polo described an amazing journey to China. In it, he mentions the young and beautiful princess Kokachin, who was to be married to the Khan of Persia and needed to be escorted to her wedding.

During the long and eventful sea voyage, which took two years, Marco Polo became like a father to the princess and he watched over her as if she were his own daughter. When they finally parted, "she wept for grief".

This is all we know about Princess Kokachin, but just imagine how her journals might have read …

March 25, 1291

I'm so excited. I can't believe what has happened. Our great leader, Kublai Khan, who rules all China and almost one-fifth of the whole world, summoned me to his palace today.

Three important messengers have arrived from Khan Arghun's court. They have travelled overland for months, all the way from Persia. What does that have

to do with me? Well, Khan Arghun's favourite wife has died, and her dying wish was that she should be replaced by someone from her own Mongol clan.

Kublai Khan wants me to be Khan Arghun's new wife! Me, Princess Kokachin! I'm only seventeen, and I'm to be married to a khan who rules all Persia! When Kublai Khan announced this to the crowded court, I blushed from head to toe.

But now I shall be leaving my homeland and going far away. I wonder if I shall ever come back to China?

June 22, 1291

This morning I watched my brothers and cousins riding across the plains.
I saw the young men shooting arrows, wrestling and playing polo. Then
I leapt on to my horse and joined them, with the wind blowing through
my hair.

We Mongols think of our horses as if they were our own legs. We have a saying, "If the horse dies, I die. If the horse lives, I live."

❧❧❧

I wonder what my life will be like in Persia. And will my husband like me?

February 11, 1292

Today Kublai Khan held a feast for thousands of people. We ate mutton and lamb, fish, wild game, eggs, vegetables, pancakes, tea, *koumiss* (fermented mare's milk) and wine, all served in golden bowls.

Then Kublai Khan introduced me to the great Venetian traveller Marco Polo, and I felt so shy, I dared not look up. Master Polo has been here in China for seventeen years and is held in great esteem.

"Marco Polo will accompany you to your wedding," said Kublai Khan, "and I shall give him two gold tablets stamped with my seal, so that you can travel freely through my kingdom." I wanted to jump for joy. Now I know I shall be safe on my long journey — but I shall be sad to say goodbye to my family. I wonder whether I shall ever see them again.

July 6, 1292

For months I have been travelling along the Grand Canal and overland, carried in a litter, just like my Chinese companion, the Sung princess. The litter rocks about and I often feel quite sick. I much prefer riding bareback!

Two days ago we arrived at the great port of Zaiton. I jumped down from the
litter and ran along the harbour, feeling the spray in my hair and the salt in my
nostrils. Then I saw the fourteen large ships Kublai Khan has made ready for us.
Each ship has four masts and lots of sails – on some I counted twelve.

I have never sailed across the sea before. I feel very nervous – but excited too!

August 14, 1292

Yesterday the seamen tested out our ship. They made a hurdle of ropes, tied a seaman to it and hoisted him into the air like a kite. The hurdle rose quickly into the wind, which means that our voyage will be successful. If the hurdle had flown badly, nobody would have wanted to set sail!

I wandered along the deck smelling the pots of herbs and ginger which we are taking with us to keep healthy. My cabin is roomy and comfortable.

My favourite rug has been draped over the bed and more rugs have been hung on the walls.

This morning we set sail. I stood on deck and watched the land grow faint in the distance. Now there is nothing but the blue-green sea. The ship rises and falls like my heartbeat.

Goodbye, China. Goodbye, home.

November 19, 1292

We've been on this ship for months, moving in a convoy, sandwiched between sea and sky.

Yesterday the wind drove our ship hither and thither, as the seamen struggled to control her. I've heard tell of six-headed creatures that search the seas for strangers; of places where the ocean boils day and night; and of a hand that reaches up out of the waves to seize passing travellers. As the gale raged, I huddled in my cabin praying to the gods. But the wind wrestled open the door and whirled me on to the deck, and a giant hand reached out of the waves to seize me!

I screamed, and Master Polo dragged me back. He carried me to my cabin, wrapping his cloak around me, and the wind did not come in search of me again.

Next day the seamen told of monsters and unicorns and an enormous whale, which rammed into the ship and broke the hull. Water poured through the cracks into some of the cabins, where everyone was soaked. That night several ships collided and were smashed. Others were lost and never seen again.

Master Polo says that soon we shall put in to shore. I do hope so.

April 17, 1293

We've been in Sumatra for almost five months now. Two thousand of us live in a fortress built by the seamen to protect us from the wild islanders. It has five wooden towers and a trench all around it leading down to the sea, where the ships are being repaired. The men keep watch from the towers and go fishing and hunting for food. But I have nothing to do but walk up and down like a caged animal.

Yesterday I persuaded Master Polo to let me go hunting, and once more I ran freely through the forests. But as we neared the mountains, we heard strange whoops and cries and the clatter of hoofs. They say that unicorns live here and men with short tails as thick as a dog's, who kill humans for food. I raced back to the fortress in fear for my life.

I hope we set sail again soon.

July 27, 1293

Hooray! We are at sea again. We've passed so many islands, I've lost count of them. On one, the people hang beautiful silks over their houses to show their wealth — but they don't wear any clothes at all! On another, the people have heads like dogs with pointed noses and sharp teeth, and they eat every stranger they meet. Luckily the sea was too rough to land. I was very pleased about that.

But we did stop at the beautiful island of Ceylon, where I met the king, who has the biggest ruby in the world. It's as thick as his wrist and glows like fire!

MEDITERRANEAN SEA

PERSIA

EGYPT

RED SEA

INDI

AFRICA

INDIAN

THE JOURNEY

- - - - - - ➤ ROUTE OF THE JOURNEY